A Treasury of
Children's
CLASSICS

Commissioning Editor   Christine Deverell
Additional Illustrations   Richard Deverell
Design   Ian Jones

©2000 Robert Frederick Limited
4-5 North Parade
Bath, U.K.
BA1 1LF

A Treasury of
Children's
CLASSICS

THREE FAIRY TALES
Adapted by
CHRISTINE DEVERELL

·CONTENTS·

Jack and the Beanstalk

ILLUSTRATED BY IVANA SVABIC CANNON

There was once a poor widow who had an only son called Jack. He was so lazy he never did any work, and as time went by, they became poorer and poorer. One fine summer's day Jack's mother decided to send him to the market to sell their cow. It was all they had left in the world and even she no longer gave them milk.

Jack had not gone very far when he met an old man. "Where are you going with that cow, young man?" said he. "I am going to the market to sell her," Jack replied. "Well, this is your lucky day," said the old man, "for I will gladly take her off your hands in exchange for these five magic beans. If you plant them, they will grow as high as the sky by tomorrow morning."

Jack thought this was a fair exchange, as it meant he could go home right away and spend the rest of the day lazing in the sun. "Look mother," he cried as he ran into the house, "I have sold our cow for these amazing beans!" "You are stupid as well as lazy," she said as she snatched the beans from his hand and threw them out of the window. Then she sent him to bed without any supper.

Jack slept until late the next morning and when he woke he

9

was not sure where he was. His room was dark, and when he opened the curtains he saw huge leaves and red flowers covering his window. He dressed himself quickly and ran downstairs and into the garden. Jack could not believe what he saw.

Just outside the window where his mother had thrown the magic beans there grew a mighty beanstalk, reaching towards the sky, so that the top of it was hidden in the clouds. Without wasting a second Jack began to climb. He climbed higher than the tree tops, higher than the clouds until he reached the blue sky and stepped out onto a long, straight, white road. Jack was very hungry by this time, so he followed the road, hoping to find a place where he could beg for some breakfast.

To his delight, he came to a castle, with a very large woman standing at the door. "Good morning," he said politely, "would you be so kind as to give me some breakfast?" "I think you had better run away as fast as you can," said the woman, "unless you want to become a breakfast yourself. My husband is an Ogre who loves nothing better than fried little boys on toast for his breakfast."

Jack was too hungry to run back along the road, so he pleaded with the woman to give him something to eat. "You can hide me from your husband when he comes," said Jack. Now the Ogre's wife was a kind woman, and she took Jack in and gave him some bread and milk. He had only just finished eating when, thump, thump, thump, he heard the Ogre walking down the road. The woman grabbed Jack and hid him in the oven.

The Ogre came into the kitchen and roared at the top of his voice: "Fee-fi-fo-fum, I smell the blood of an Englishman. Be he alive, or be he dead, I'll grind his bones to make my bread." "Nonsense!" said the wife, "you are always saying you can smell Englishmen. Now sit down and have your breakfast." Jack peeped out of his hiding place and was terrified to see what a

huge, ugly monster he was. The table was piled high with food
and the Ogre ate all of it.

Then he called to his wife, "Bring me my bags of gold!" She
cleared the table and put the gold in front of him. There he sat
counting and counting the coins until his eyelids began to droop
and his head nodded slowly down and rested on the table; he fell
fast asleep, snoring so loudly that people on the earth below
thought they heard a thunderstorm.

When Jack peeped out and saw all that gold he knew this was his big chance. He crept out of the oven, and as he passed the sleeping Ogre Jack reached up and grabbed one of the bags of gold. He ran away from the castle and down the straight, white road as fast as his legs would carry him, back to the top of the beanstalk. He climbed down through the green leaves until he reached his own little garden again.

14

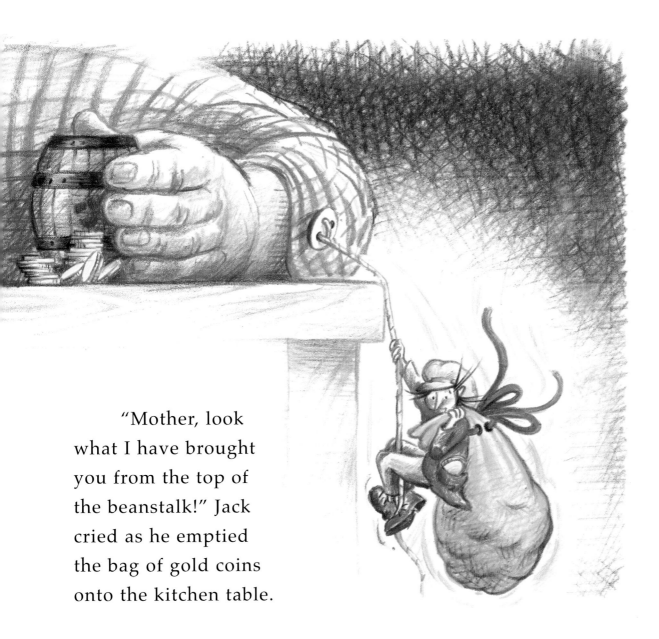

"Mother, look what I have brought you from the top of the beanstalk!" Jack cried as he emptied the bag of gold coins onto the kitchen table.

The poor widow was pleased to have her son home again, and now they had money to buy all they needed.

One day, Jack took out the bag and saw that there was not much gold left, so he decided to climb the beanstalk again. He disguised himself so that the woman would not recognise him, and once again she let him in and gave him some food.

The Ogre returned to the castle in the evening and Jack hid in a huge copper pot. Then he called to his wife to bring him his golden hen. The wife brought the hen and placed it on the table. "Lay!" roared the Ogre, and the hen laid an egg of solid gold. "Lay another!" and the hen laid an even larger golden egg. When Jack saw the golden eggs his eyes popped out of his head.

Soon, the Ogre fell asleep at the table and when Jack was sure that no one else was about, he climbed out of the copper pot and grabbed the Ogre's hen.

The hen started
to squawk as Jack ran
towards the door, and
the Ogre woke up.
A few seconds passed before he
realised that the hen was not on the
table, and when he looked out of the
window, he saw Jack with his prize
bird under his arm, running for all he
was worth along the straight white
road. The Ogre chased after Jack
with huge strides. The people
in the world below
thought that they could
hear an earthquake.
Even though Jack was
running faster than he had
ever run in his life, the Ogre
was almost upon him when
Jack reached the beanstalk.

Just as the Ogre reached out his hand to grab Jack and retrieve his precious hen, Jack slipped nimbly down the beanstalk. The Ogre paused for a few moments, wondering if this strange plant would carry his weight. Then he began to climb slowly down after Jack. The beanstalk began to sway and creak, and Jack, realising the Ogre was following, went even faster. When Jack reached his garden he called out, "Quick! Quick! Get me an axe, mother!"

He seized the axe, handed her the golden hen, and began to chop at the mighty beanstalk. It swayed and creaked and then it fell with a tremendous crash!

The Ogre lay dead under the leaves. Jack and his mother lived happily all their lives with the golden hen, that brought them more riches than they knew how to spend.

Cinderella

I L L U S T R A T E D   B Y   B R I A N   R O B E R T S O N

Once upon a time a rich gentleman who was sad after the death of his wife, decided to marry again, so his lovely daughter could have a mother to care for her.

Unfortunately he chose a proud and selfish woman with two daughters just like herself. She did not reveal her true character until after the wedding. She ordered the little girl to work in the kitchen and live with the servants, while she and her daughters enjoyed a life of splendour.

When the child had finished her work, she used to sit in the chimney corner among the cinders; so everyone called her Cinderella. Her clothes were dirty and ragged, but she was far prettier than her sisters in all their fine clothes.

One day an invitation arrived from the palace. The King's son was giving a ball! The sisters could not have been happier. They talked of nothing but what they would wear, and ordered beautiful gowns from the best dressmakers in the land. Cinderella would have loved to go to the ball, and the wicked sisters teased her mercilessly saying; "Wouldn't you just love to dress up in these fine clothes and ride in a carriage to the palace, and dance with rich young men, and maybe even with the Prince himself?"

22

It was known that the Prince was in search of a wife, and Cinderella's mean stepmother had high hopes for her daughters. Soon, the great day arrived. Cinderella was busy all day, dressing her sisters, polishing their shoes, combing their hair, and when the splendid carriage arrived to take them to the ball, she dutifully arranged their gowns so they would not crumple on the journey.

When they were out of sight, Cinderella sat down alone and exhausted in the chimney corner and began to cry. Then, all of a sudden, her Fairy Godmother appeared and said, "Why are you crying?" "I wish I could go to the ball," sobbed Cinderella. "Well then, be a good girl and do as I say. And you shall go to the ball! Run along to the garden and bring me a pumpkin."

Cinderella found the biggest and best pumpkin and brought it to her Fairy Godmother who touched it with her magic wand. Instantly it became a beautiful golden coach. "Now bring me the mouse-trap, and open it very carefully."

Six mice ran out of the trap, and as the Fairy Godmother touched each one with her wand, it turned into a fine dapple grey horse. Cinderella was then sent to find a rat for her Fairy Godmother to turn into a handsome postilion, and six lizards which became smart footmen.

"Well now, will that be fit to carry a lady to the ball?" asked the Fairy Godmother. "Oh yes. It's wonderful," replied Cinderella, "but . . ."

"Aha! You're wondering what you are going to wear, are you not? Let's see; what would suit you?" With these words, she waved her wand over Cinderella, and in an instant her rags became the most magnificent dress you can imagine. She was wearing the most costly jewels in the world, and on her feet was a beautiful pair of glass slippers. "Off you go now," said the Fairy Godmother, "but mind you leave the palace before the clock strikes twelve, or all this magic will be undone."

Cinderella promised to obey, and set off in her golden carriage. When she appeared in the ballroom, everyone fell silent and the music and dancing stopped, for she was the most beautiful young woman in the room. The young Prince took her hand and led her out to dance with him. He danced with no one else the whole evening.

When they sat down to the feast, he was so busy looking at her that he did not eat a thing! The dancing continued. Cinderella was so happy, she had danced every dance and did not feel tired. Then she heard a clock striking the hour. "It must be 11 o'clock. It cannot possibly be midnight yet," she said to herself, mindful of her Fairy Godmother's warning.

But as she turned and saw the clock, Cinderella gasped with fright and ran as fast as she could from the ballroom. The Prince tried to catch up with her as the clock continued to chime.

As she ran through the door and down the steps towards the golden carriage, she lost one of her glass slippers, and at the very moment that the Prince bent down to retrieve it, the clock struck twelve. As he stood up, the Prince did not see a sign of his beautiful dancing partner; and the coach and horses had completely vanished. Behind a hedge in the garden sat poor Cinderella in her ragged, dirty clothes.

Beside her was the pumpkin; and the mice, the rat and the lizards scurried away. When she was certain that the Prince had gone, Cinderella made her way

home on foot as fast as she could.   The
music and dancing would have continued until morning, but the
Prince was in no mood for celebration, and all the guests were
sent away. He took the glass slipper to the King and said, "I will
find the maiden whose foot this slipper fits, and when I have

found her, she will be my bride." Cinderella's stepmother grew very excited when the Prince arrived at their house. "It's only a shoe," she said to her daughters; "one of you will be able to squeeze your foot into it." But they tried in vain. It was a tiny, dainty slipper, and the sisters had big, clumsy feet. "Are there any other young women in this house?" asked the Prince. "Only Cinderella," said the mother, "but she works in the kitchen, and we didn't take her to the ball." "Bring her here," demanded the Prince. And when Cinderella tried on the slipper everyone cried, "It fits! It fits!" The stepmother and her daughters were white with rage.

The Prince looked

31

into Cinderella's eyes and recognised that she was indeed the beautiful stranger he had danced with, and he took her away to be his bride. They lived happily for many years in the great palace, and the Princess, who later became Queen, was always kind to her servants, and invited them to attend the annual ball.

Snow White & the Seven Dwarfs

I L L U S T R A T E D   B Y   D A V I D   L O N G

It was the middle of winter. A Queen sat by a window made of the finest black ebony. As she looked out at the snow, she pricked her finger and three drops of blood fell onto it.

She gazed at the red drops in the white snow and said, "I wish my little daughter to be as white as the snow, as red as blood and as black as ebony ."

And her daughter was beautiful, with skin as white as snow, cheeks as rosy as the blood, and hair as black as ebony. Her name was Snow White.

Sadly the Queen died, and Snow White's father married another wife. This Queen had a magic mirror. She would gaze at herself and say,

"Mirror, mirror, on the wall,
　　Who is the fairest of them all?"
And the mirror would reply,
　　"You, O Queen, are the fairest in
　　　the land."

But one day, when she looked into the mirror, it answered her,

"You my Queen, may lovely be
But Snow White is by far the most beautiful in the land."

The Queen called one of her servants and ordered him to take Snow White out into the woods. "I never want to see her again", she screeched!

The servant was very unhappy and did not want to hurt Snow White. So he left her in the wood, and returned to the Queen to tell her that Snow White was dead.

Poor Snow White was alone and afraid as she wandered in the wood. As night fell, she reached a cottage.

It was the home of seven dwarfs. Inside, she found a table neatly laid with seven small loaves of bread and seven little glasses of wine. Against the wall were seven small beds.

Snow White was very hungry, so she helped herself to a little bread from each loaf, and a sip of wine from each glass. Then she lay down and fell asleep.

When they returned from their day's work, the seven dwarfs were not at all pleased with the mess that they saw on the table.

They turned around and found Snow White sleeping soundly.

At first they grumbled and complained to one another, but then, they all gazed in amazement at her beauty, and agreed to let her sleep until morning.

Snow White stayed with the dwarfs. While they were hard at work in the Diamond Mine, she looked after their cottage and prepared the meals every day. One day, the Queen looked into her mirror and asked her usual question.

The mirror replied;

"You are the fairest in this place.
But by far the most beautiful face
Belongs to Snow White."

The Queen was furious. "I thought she was
dead!" she cried. She disguised herself
as an old gypsy woman and went
off into the woods in search of
Snow White. She carried
with her a basket of
apples. One of the
apples was poisoned
on one side. When
she came upon the
cottage, she knocked
on the door.

Snow White
opened the window,
looked out and said,
"I dare not let anyone in."

"Never mind dear. Just let me give you one of my beautiful apples." Snow White did not want to take it, but the Queen said, "Look, I will take a bite and you will see that it is safe."

Snow White then took a bite of the apple and fell down dead. When the dwarfs returned from work that day they were very unhappy to find Snow White lying lifeless on the ground. She was so beautiful and they wanted to look at her forever, so they laid her in a glass coffin.

Snow White looked as if she were only sleeping. One day a prince rode by and begged the dwarfs to let him take Snow White away with him. They refused at first, but then they took pity on him, and granted his wish. As soon as he lifted the coffin, a piece of apple fell from Snow White's lips, and she awoke.

The Prince asked Snow White to go with him to his father's palace and marry him.

The wicked Queen was invited to the marriage feast, and when she arrived and saw that Snow White was the bride, she choked with rage, fell ill and died. But Snow White and the Prince reigned happily over that land for many, many years.